THE CASE OF THE
ELEVATOR
DUCK

by Polly Berrien Berends
illustrated by Diane Allison

A STEPPING STONE BOOK™
Random House 🏠 New York

With special thanks to
E.F. and S.A.

Originally published by Random House in 1973. First Stepping Stone edition, 1989.
Text copyright © 1973 by Polly Berrien Berends, copyright renewed 2001 by Polly
Berrien Berends. Illustrations copyright © 1989 by Diane Allison. Cover illustration
copyright © 2004 by Rachel Isadora. All rights reserved under International and
Pan-American Copyright Conventions. Published in the United States by Random
House Children's Books, a division of Random House, Inc., New York, and
simultaneously in Canada by Random House of Canada Limited, Toronto.

www.randomhouse.com/kids

Library of Congress Cataloging-in-Publication Data
Berends, Polly Berrien. The case of the elevator duck / by Polly Berrien Berends ;
illustrated by Diane Allison.
 p. cm. — (A Stepping stone book)
SUMMARY: Chronicles the adventures of an eleven-year-old detective that result
from finding a duck in the elevator of his apartment building.
ISBN 0-394-82646-9 (pbk.) — ISBN 0-394-92646-3 (lib. bdg.)
[1. City and town life—Fiction.] I. Allison, Diane Worfolk, ill. II. Title.
PZ7.B4482Cas 1989 [Fic]—dc19 88-23971

Printed in the United States of America 33

RANDOM HOUSE and colophon are registered trademarks and A STEPPING STONE
BOOK and colophon are trademarks of Random House, Inc.

Contents

1

A Duck Out of Water

On weekends and evenings and vacations I am a detective. I do not wear a disguise. I do not need disguises because I am only eleven years old. Nobody suspects an eleven-year-old boy of being a detective. My name is Gilbert. I live in a housing project. I live in 12H.

Someday I am going to be a full-time detective. So for now I practice every chance I get. For instance, I make it my business to ride the elevator. This is the best way to keep track of who comes and goes. In our building everyone comes and goes by the elevators— except sometimes the people on the second floor use the fire stairs.

Two days ago at 8:15 A.M. I step into an Up elevator. I ride alone to the top floor—the 25th. I do not get off. The elevator goes down. It stops at nearly every floor. As usual at 8:15 the elevator is jammed by the time we reach the 17th floor. There is a lot of pushing and grunting. I think I will be crushed to death by this fat lady in front of me. But I do not say anything. Probably she is thinking she will be crushed by the man in front of her. Besides I think we will all die anyway from this other man's stinking cigar.

Finally the elevator reaches the lobby and everyone gets off. Everyone except me. Now is when I head back to 12H for breakfast. I make my move. As the lady in front of me gets off I step to the front of the elevator and press close to the wall where the self-service buttons are. I wait nervously for the doors to

close. I do not like anyone to notice that I stay on the elevator. I do not want people getting wise to me.

The doors close. No one has seen me. I push the 12 button and get ready to relax. Then it happens. I get this feeling. I know that I am not alone. Slowly I turn my head to one side. I look out of the corner of one eye. I am right. I am not alone. There is a duck in the elevator with me. A white duck with orange feet.

Ducks are not allowed in our building. No Pets of Any Sort are allowed in the projects. So if anyone gets on this elevator now and sees me and this duck together, I am going to be in bad trouble. It is not easy to get into the projects—especially a low-income project like ours. The rent is low and they've got plenty of water and heat and all. You have to show need before you can even get on the waiting list. We waited two years before our number came up.

"No way!" I say to the duck. "I am not going to get us kicked out of here for no duck no how."

I look away. If anybody does get onto the elevator, he will not see me paying any attention to any duck.

But the elevator goes straight to 12 without stopping. The doors open and I dash out. I am safe. I will go and have my breakfast in peace, and the elevator will carry the duck to some other floor.

And then what? Who will find that duck next? What if it's the Housing Inspector? What if it's somebody that likes to eat duck?

I turn around and look into the elevator. The duck is just standing there on these ridiculous orange feet—looking at me.

As the doors start to close, the dumb duck quacks. I can't stand it. I stick my arms through the closing doors just in time. The doors open. I grab the duck and charge down the hall. Ducks are not my usual line of work. But I don't have anything against them either. And I just don't like the idea of anyone cooking a duck that has looked me straight in the eye and quacked.

"O.K., Easter," I say, "I'll take your case."

2
Webfooted Friend

I call him Easter because I figure he is probably some kid's leftover Easter present. Easter was a long time ago, but that's the only time we ever get ducks coming into our neighborhood. At Easter there are always a lot of guys around selling baby ducks and chicks and bunnies from the country. They go for a couple of dollars, and most of them get sold to aunts and uncles who like to make kids smile but who will not be around to see what happens next. What happens next is that after a few days most of the animals die. And the children cry. But by the next Easter nobody remembers that.

It is almost September. Next week I will go back to school. I figure Easter the duck must be special if he has managed to stay alive in the city all the way from Easter to September.

Maybe one reason he is still alive is because he is good at keeping quiet. When I get into 12H I put him into the laundry hamper until I can have a talk with my mother. I peek through the air holes in the side of the hamper. The duck just sits there peeking back at me, not making any noise at all. Maybe he is stupid or maybe it's just that he isn't a quacker. My mother says that I am still waters that run deep. I guess she means I think a lot even though I don't say much. Maybe Easter is like that.

Probably Easter is still alive because somebody who really loves him has been taking good care of him. I think it is important to find that somebody.

I explain all this to my mother at breakfast. I tell her how Easter quacked me straight in the eye. But she does not like the idea of a duck in our apartment one bit.

"We wait two years to get into the projects," she says, "and now you bring home a duck. A duck! If the housing police catch us with a duck in our apartment, we will all be out on the street. No, Gilbert, I won't have it!"

I take my mother's hand and lead her into the bathroom. I lift up the lid of the hamper.

"Look, Mama," I say.

We both look. Easter is still sitting there—real quiet—on my striped pajamas. He tips his head to one side and looks up at Mama. Maybe this is the only way a duck can look up, but it is still a pretty cute thing to do.

Mama puts the lid back down on the hamper and steers me by the head back to the kitchen.

"If your father were here—" she says, and I know then that I'm home free. My father isn't here. He's in the merchant marines and

he won't be home again until the end of next month.

Mama gives me three days to find Easter's owner. I tell her I think she is a pretty cool lady. She is.

3

Ruffled Feathers

After breakfast Mama and I move Easter into
the bathtub. We do not know anything about
ducks, but we give him some water and some
rolled oats. He takes a little of both. Then he
makes a mess in the bottom of the tub and
starts cleaning himself with his bill. I guess
he feels at home. While I am cleaning up the
tub he comes over and pushes my arm. What
do you know—he's even friendly!

I would like to stay and play with him, but

three days is not very long and I better get busy. Easter pulls out one of his wing feathers. I pick it up and start thinking.

First I ask myself what are the facts. I am pretty sure Easter is a lost duck and not a ducknapped one. After all, nobody would go to all the trouble of stealing a duck and then leave it in the elevator.

No, I am pretty sure Easter just walked into that elevator himself. I also think he is a project duck. Even Easter could not have walked through our neighborhood and stayed alive. The dogs would have gotten him. Or the cats. Or the kids. So Easter must be a lost project duck, who happened to wander out of somebody's apartment and into the elevator. Maybe he was following his owner.

I also know that whoever lost Easter loves and misses him very much. Anyone who would dare to hide a duck in the projects would have to be either crazy or in love with the duck. I mean, who wants to get kicked out on account of a duck? This thought reminds me I better get busy.

The doorbell rings. I answer and it's—*bonk,*

bonk—Dennis Herter. Dennis says "hey" all the time, and just like now he is always bouncing a basketball and sort of nodding his head in a cool way.

"You wanna shoot a few, Gilbert?" he says. "Hey, you wanna?"

"No, man," I say. "I'd like to, but I can't today. I'm on a case."

"On a case, hey?" says Dennis. "Sure, sure. Big detective."

He shuffles off down the hall, bouncing his ball. *Bonk, bonk, bonk.* Dennis always talks

tough and like he couldn't care less. Actually we are very good friends.

It is nearly noon when I walk out of 12H. I am still carrying Easter's wing feather and I still do not have any idea of where to look for his owner. I cannot put a note on the bulletin board in the laundry room because nobody in the projects, including me, is going to admit to having anything to do with a duck. I also can't just go from door to door asking because you never know who is going to report you to the Housing Inspector. Besides,

there are too many apartments for me to check in three days.

At 12:15 I step into the Down elevator. This is what I always do at noon—just to see who comes and goes. Besides, since I haven't a better plan, I think it is best to start looking for Easter's owner at the scene of the crime—where I found him, I mean.

At this time of day the elevator is usually empty going down and full going up. Today is no different. It is on the way down that I get two ideas.

My first idea is that I will look for familiar faces from this morning's run. Easter did not ring for the elevator by himself, so he must have gotten on with somebody else. Maybe that somebody saw him get on? I am not too hopeful about this idea.

Then suddenly this really cool idea pops into my head. It's about Easter's wing feather. I take off my belt and put it around my head. Then I stick the feather into the back of the belt. To most people I will just look like any other kid playing Indian. But to Easter's owner I hope I will look like somebody with one of Easter's feathers.

As usual at lunchtime the Up elevator is full of women who have been grocery shopping or who only work half days. I do not see anyone from the 8:15 run. They are mostly nine-to-five workers who don't come home until around 6:00. Nobody pays any attention to me and my duck feather.

I spend most of the afternoon wandering around the building, hoping that the right person will see me in my duck feather and ask about Easter. At 3:35 P.M. I even try hitting my hand over my mouth and yelling "woo-woo-woo" at the top of my lungs in the laundry room. But all that happens is that this skinny lady tells me, "Look, kid, if you want to play Indians go out on the playground where you belong."

I follow the skinny lady's suggestion and try my woo-woo-woo approach on the playground. This time I am noticed all right, but all that happens is some little kids start yelling "woo-woo-woo," too, and "bang-bang-you're-dead." They just want to play cowboys and Indians.

By this time I am fairly discouraged so I decide to go along with the game for a while. I think I am too old to be playing cowboys and Indians but that this is as good a way as any to advertise Easter's feather.

I have just been shot and am comfortably playing dead by the sandbox, thinking that it's too bad to outgrow things, when the worst happens. I hear this *bonk, bonk, bonk* sound next to my ear. I open my eyes and it's Dennis Herter standing over me, shaking his head.

"On a case, hey?" he says. "Too busy to shoot baskets? Too young is more like it."

"Yeah! No kidding!" I say. "I'm working now. This is all part of my plan."

I can see he doesn't believe me, but I don't try to argue. I mean, what's the point?

At 5:00 P.M. I am still playing cowboys and Indians. About this time people start picking up kids from the Day Care Center. All these little kids who have working mothers go by on their way home. I think for a minute that this one sad-eyed little kid is watching me. Maybe he is looking at my duck feather? I go over to him hopefully, but he just runs along after his big sister.

It's about time for me to head back to the elevators. Pretty soon the nine-to-five workers will be coming home, including the ones that were with Easter and me in the elevator this morning.

This time I do not get on the elevator. There are two elevators. I do not want to be up in one while the somebody who got on with Easter this morning goes up in the other. I stay in the lobby until 6:30 P.M. I recognize five faces from this morning. This proves that all my detective practice is working. Of the five people I recognize, I manage to speak to four about Easter. Well, I don't exactly mention Easter. I just ask if they noticed anything unusual in the elevator this morning. Or if they lost anything. They didn't. At least the four people I speak to didn't.

By 6:30 the lobby is empty. A few people are still coming in, but I give up and decide to go home for supper. I push the button for the elevator. When it comes, there is this same sad-eyed kid in it. I hold the door for him to get off, but he just stands there.

I say, "Don't you want to get off?"

But he keeps standing there. Well, I figure he is just a little kid who likes to ride elevators. I can understand that. I sort of dig them myself. So I push the 12 button and head for home. All the way up this kid keeps looking at me. He doesn't say anything. Once he sort of smiles, but mostly he just keeps looking at me out of the saddest eyes you ever

saw. Even after I get off at 12 I keep seeing
those sad eyes in my mind.

Nothing much more happens that day. I
fool around with Easter in the bathroom, but
I don't do any more detective work. It's not
that I'm lazy. It's just that I don't have any
more ideas. I have two more nights and two
more days left to find Easter's owner. But I
don't have any more ideas.

I ask my mother what will happen if I don't find Easter's owner. She says we will have to take him to an animal shelter. I know what that means. The End. Nobody in this city is going to adopt a full-grown duck, so the shelter will put him to sleep. Forever.

4

Dead Duck?

Things go just as badly the next morning, and I am feeling cross and tired when I come home for lunch. I open the door and see my mother looking scared. In the living room are two men. One is a housing policeman. I can tell by his uniform. The other is the Housing Inspector. He is carrying a clipboard.

Now I know what is wrong with Mama. Once in a while the Housing Inspector goes through the apartments in the projects. He is

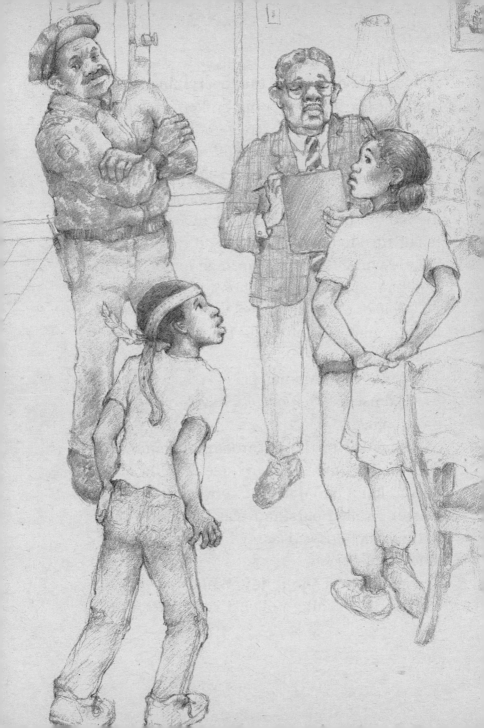

supposed to make sure that everything is clean and that no rules are being broken. He checks that you don't have extra people living with you. No air conditioners. No Pets of Any Sort. Anything like that is called an Infraction of the Housing Regulations and you can get kicked out of the projects for it. Right now it is our turn to be inspected. And right now we have a white-feathered, orange-footed infraction named Easter in our bathtub! Not cool!

"You don't mind if we just have a quick look around, do you?" the Housing Inspector is saying.

"Well," says Mama.

"Excuse me," I say. "I have to go to the bathroom."

I make it to the bathroom, slamming the door behind me. Easter quacks hello and I cough loud and hard to cover up. I take Easter's rolled oats and water and put them in the linen closet. Easter I put into the hamper.

Next I flush the toilet. While the toilet is making its flushing noise, I run water in the bathtub and wash Easter's latest messes down the drain.

"Now, be quiet," I whisper into the hamper.

Then I walk back into the living room—real slow—whistling a little.

Mama keeps our apartment cleaner than anybody's, so the Housing Inspector does not look very hard. Just the same my heart is pounding like mad when he sticks his head into our bathroom. I mean, just suppose Easter decides to quack hello to *him!*

But good old Easter doesn't say anything. Pretty soon the Housing Inspector and the policeman go away.

I am in the middle of rescuing Easter from the hamper when Mama comes in and starts giving me her mad look. One night about two months ago two big guys shook me upside down to see if I had any money in my pockets and then gave me a black eye because I didn't. Mama is looking at me now the same way she did when she saw my black eye. Actually it's a scared look. I know she isn't really mad.

"I'm sorry, Mama," I tell her.

She tells me she's sorry, too. She says she knows she gave me three days to find Easter's owner, but she has changed her mind. It is too dangerous to keep a duck around. She doesn't know what we would do if we got thrown out of the projects. Neither do I. She says if I don't find Easter's owner by tomorrow morning, we will have to take him to the animal shelter.

We sit on the edge of the bathtub together and watch Easter. When he walks, his orange feet make this ridiculous slapping sound on the bottom of the tub. He already seems like part of the family. Mama likes him, too. I can see that she feels terrible. I hug her.

"It's all right, Mama," I tell her. "I understand."

But I don't understand. I mean, I don't see why it's anybody else's business if you want to have a duck in your apartment—or an ant-eater—or anything. Just so long as it's in *your* apartment and doesn't bother anyone else.

5

Hatching a Plan

I do not argue with Mama about the three days getting cut short. By now I think I am a lousy detective and I don't see what good an extra day will do anyway.

All afternoon I wear my feather around the project. Nobody notices me except Dennis Herter, who says, "Still playing cowboys and Indians, hey? Man, you are something else!"

I don't even try to defend myself.

Evening comes and I still don't have any

new ideas about how to find Easter's owner.
Mama and I are really down at supper.

After supper I say that I think I will go
and take my bath now. This is a mistake.
Mama knows right away how awful I am feeling if I do such a weird thing as taking a bath
without being told.

While I am in the bath Easter walks up
and down the edge of the tub, slapping his
feet. I invite him to come in for a swim, but
this only seems to upset him. He walks back
and forth, quacking and nodding his head up

and down. Maybe it's just that he doesn't like warm water. Still I get the idea he sort of knows he's supposed to swim, but that he doesn't know how. If I could keep him, I would teach him to swim.

At bedtime it really hits me. Tomorrow morning it's The End for Easter. Here I am supposed to be some great detective and I haven't done anything. I figure the least I can do is to use my head a little.

On a real case, a robbery for example, I would try to think like a thief. But this is no robbery. It is not even a ducknapping. Easter is not stolen. Easter is lost. All right then, I will think like a duck and see where that gets me.

This is easier said than done. I do not know anything about ducks, and Easter is the only duck I know.

Then I remember from school that wild ducks migrate. They fly hundreds and hundreds of miles to the same place every winter. They can do that because they have an amazing sense of direction.

Easter is not a wild duck. Easter is a

domesticated duck, like from a farm. And he is a city duck at that—a duck that probably doesn't even know how to swim. Even if domesticated ducks are supposed to have a good sense of direction like wild ducks, the chances are that Easter hasn't learned how to use his. But it's an idea. It's a long shot, but there isn't much time left. A long shot is better than no shot at all.

I do not tell Mama my plan because I do not want to get her hopes up for nothing. Also I do not want her to say no. I just kiss her good-night. Then I go to the bathroom and say good-night to Easter. I say it loud so Mama can hear. But then I whisper, "See you later," to Easter.

Before getting into bed I slip this old hand mirror into my bathrobe pocket. Then I take my ball of pieces of string down from the closet shelf. It is a good thing I save string because I am going to need it for my plan. I put the string under my pillow, set the alarm clock for 1:00 A.M., and climb into bed.

I am not at all sleepy, but that is all right because I still have a few details to think out.

Basically my plan is to see if Easter can find his own way home. I know this sounds crazy, but it is the only thing I can think of left to try.

At 11:00 Mama comes in and kisses me on the cheek. After that I fall asleep for a while. Then suddenly I wake up. I have trained myself to wake up when the alarm gives this little click just before it goes off. I push the button down just in time. I am wide awake and the alarm has not sounded.

I put on my slippers and my bathrobe. Then I take the string from under my pillow and go to the bathroom. I do not know if Easter has been asleep or not, but when I open the door his shiny little eyes are wide open. He looks very with it. I think this is a good sign.

"Keep quiet," I tell him. But I do not worry because by this time I trust him to be quiet when quietness is important. I tiptoe to the front door carrying Easter and my ball of pieces of string. I take the apartment key from the magnetic hook on the door. Then I let myself out into the hall.

6

Sitting Ducks

I have to admit that I am a little afraid. Partly it's that I have never been out this late before in my life. Partly it is because I do not know what in the world I will do if I meet someone. But it's a choice between this and The End. So I do not hesitate.

I go straight to the elevator and push the Up button. I stand with my back against the wall next to the elevator. The elevator comes and the doors open. I hold out my hand mirror and look at it to see into the elevator. Luckily it is empty. I step quickly inside and push 25.

At 25 we get off. I carry Easter to the end of the hall and push open the door to the fire stairs. There I put him down and tie the string to one of his orange legs.

My idea is to take him to each floor and see if he recognizes any apartment. I do not dare to take the elevator. Even in the middle of the night there are always people coming and going in our building. One of these people is the housing policeman, and I sure don't want to meet *him*—not in my pajamas in the middle of the night with a duck on a string! This is why I have decided to use the fire stairs. I will lead Easter down the stairs. I will open the door to each floor and see if he seems at home anywhere.

I unroll a lot of string and open the door to the 25th floor. Easter only tips his head to one side and looks up at me in that cute way of his. Either 25 is not where he lives or else he doesn't know how to use his sense of direction. I wish I knew which. It is a long way to the lobby.

But I am not going to give up yet. I start down the stairs toward the next floor. Easter follows. For a duck he is pretty good at going down stairs. His orange legs are not long enough to reach the steps one foot at a time. So he jumps with both feet at once and lands on each step with a loud double slap.

He does not show any interest in the 24th floor. Or in the next. Or in the next. On the way to 21 I get the idea that he is tired. I can tell because he keeps sitting down on about every third step. So from now on I carry him and only put him down when I open the door to each floor.

He is not at all excited by either of the next two floors. When I put him down on 19 and open the door, I think he recognizes something. He takes a few steps and then stops. I think maybe this is it! But after that nothing more happens and pretty soon I pick him up again. Then I see that he has only made a mess on the floor.

"Thanks, pal," I say. I am really grateful that he didn't make his mess between floors—in my arms, I mean.

I am just starting down to the next floor when I see that I am about to make a big mistake. I thought nobody ever used the fire stairs, especially this high up in our building. After all, they are only there in case of fire. But from the landing on 19 I can see this man

and woman hugging each other on the land-ing of 18.

There is nothing to do but sit down and wait. Good old Easter falls asleep in my lap. I am so tired that I could sleep too, except that it is freezing cold in the stairway. I sit there shivering for a long time.

I begin to have serious doubts about my plan. I feel almost sure that we have already passed Easter's floor and that he just doesn't know how to use his sense of direction. It has taken at least 45 minutes to go six floors. There are still eighteen to go. And it doesn't look as if the man and woman on 18 are ever going to stop hugging each other and go home.

I am just thinking of quitting and going home myself when the door on 18 opens. I hear this voice say, "All right, you two. Break it up."

I peek through the railing to see who it is. It is the housing policeman. I am glad be-cause now the man and woman go inside. But I am very nervous because I did not know be-fore that the housing policeman checked the stairway. Next time he checks he will probably catch me and Easter.

But I decide to go on. I wake up Easter and carry him down to 18. I peek through the window, but the man and woman and the policeman have gone. I open the door. 18 is not Easter's floor. Neither is 17. And neither is 16.

On the next floor I make a big decision. I am cold and I am tired. I do not know if Easter will recognize his floor even if we come to it. So I decide that if nothing happens by the time we get to my floor—12—I will give up and go home.

Nothing happens on 15 or 14. By the time we reach 13, I have lost all hope. I am nearly in tears and I am hugging Easter almost to death. All the same I put him down on 13 and open the door.

What do you know about that! He walks right in. He is walking straight down the hall of the 13th floor, slapping his great big silly orange feet! As fast as I can I unroll my ball of pieces of string.

Easter stops in front of 13B and quacks. 13B is way at the other end of the hall. I cannot be at all sure that this is where he lives, but at this point I have nothing to lose. Neither does Easter.

So I tiptoe down the hall and cut the string from Easter's leg. I ring the doorbell of 13B

hard, three times. Then as fast as I can I run back to the stairway.

I peek through the window. Nothing happens. I am just about to give up hope when the door of 13B opens. I could faint when I see who is at the door! It is that quiet kid with the sad eyes that I've been seeing every-

where. Only now he is talking about a mile a minute. His eyes are sparkling like crazy and he is hugging Easter and sort of laughing and crying all at once.

"So long, Easter," I whisper. Then I rush down the stairs to the 12th floor and let myself into 12H. I think I must be really tired because for some reason I am crying, too.

7

Just Ducky

As usual at 8:15 A.M. I step into the Up elevator for my morning run. The elevator is empty going up and it is the same as always going down—the crowding, the pushing, the grunting. Today there is no man with a stinking cigar. There is this lady with garlic breath. I think garlic breath is worse than the cigar.

But I am feeling good. I am glad about Easter and I am glad to be back on the job. Maybe now I'll pick up a more routine case—

a mugging or something. Today I feel I could handle anything. But maybe I'll just hunt up Dennis Herter and shoot a few baskets for a change.

Everyone except me gets off at the main floor. I step up out of sight by the self-service buttons as usual. No one sees me. The doors close and I head home for breakfast.

Then it happens. I get this feeling again. I know that I am not alone. Slowly I turn my head to one side and look out of the corner of my eye. I am right. I am not alone. Easter is in there with me.

I am boiling mad. I love Easter. I care about what happens to him. I have gone to a whole lot of trouble to get him back to his owner. It burns me up that that sad-eyed kid has let Easter get lost in the elevator again, the very next day after he has come home.

I push the 13 button. The elevator stops at 12, but I do not get off. I get off at 13 and go straight to 13B and ring the buzzer. I keep ringing and ringing until this girl answers. I am just about to give her a piece of my mind when *she* begins giving *me* a piece of hers. Too much!

I am speechless at this. I stand there holding Easter while this girl actually bawls me out for bringing him home!

She speaks with a Spanish accent. She tells me to get "thees dawk out of here." She says it belongs to her little brother. He got it for Easter last spring when they were still living in a tenement.

She says they finally got a chance to move into the projects. They have only been in America a year. Her parents do not speak any English. They do not understand about No Pets of Any Sort in the lease. The Inspector tells them to get rid of the duck. But they do not understand. They do not get rid of the duck. So the Inspector makes it very clear. If the duck does not go, they will be thrown out of the projects.

Her little brother is very sad. He is shy. He does not speak any English. The duck is his only friend in America. He is heartbroken that he must send his duck away. He does not have any idea of how to find a new home for his duck. So he puts it on the elevator. He figures everyone rides the elevator. He hopes someone who will love the duck will take him home.   .

All this time I am listening. I am not angry anymore, but this girl is still furious.

"Two days ago," she said, "he come home a little bit happy. He say this nice boy take his duck home. He is sad still, but he feel glad because his duck have a good home. And then you bring him back! Why? So this morning my little brother can cry some more and put his duck on the elevator again? What's the matter with you? You want to break a little boy's heart?"

What can I say? I say, "Please let me explain."

But she will not listen. She says she must take her little brother to the Day Care Center now. He is putting on his coat this very minute. She pushes me away from the door. She says to go away quickly because she does not want her little brother to see his duck again.

So I go. What else can I do? I hide Easter
under my sweater and get onto the elevator.
I push 12 and start trying to think up what I
will tell Mama.

Then I get this idea. I think I am going to
go crazy from having so many ideas.

Once again I do not get off at 12. I go all
the way back to the main floor. I walk straight
through the lobby and out the front door with

Easter under my sweater. At this point I am so mad that I don't much care who sees me with Easter.

I walk around to the back of the building and push open the door marked Day Care Center. I walk into the office and say that I want to see the head teacher.

This lady behind the desk says she is the teacher and would I care to sit down. I shut the door and start sounding off. I am not much of a talker except when I am mad. Now I am plenty mad. I tell her the whole story.

By the time the girl from 13B gets to the Center with her little brother, everything is all set and I am waiting in the playroom with the teacher.

The teacher asks the girl to wait a minute. She sits down and looks at me in this kind of surprised way. When all the other kids get there, the teacher calls the sad-eyed kid to her side. She whispers to him and points at me. By the time she stops talking, he is smiling and nodding like crazy.

She sends the kid over to me. I take Easter

out from under my sweater and give him to
the kid. Before I can stop him, he gives me
this huge wet kiss.

The teacher tells the rest of the class that
Julio, the sad-eyed kid, is going to share his
duck with all the children at the Day Care
Center. Easter will be a Day Care duck and
Julio will be in charge of him.

Pretty soon I leave. The kid is still smiling and trying to talk to the other children, who are all crowding around him. He is going to have lots of friends now, and Easter has a good safe home at last.

I am just heading back up to 12H for breakfast when this girl steps into the elevator with me. She is not angry anymore. She is blushing.

"My name is Rita," she says. "I am sorry—"

"Skip it," I tell her. "I understand."

About the Author

POLLY BERRIEN BERENDS says, "When I was a child, I liked books that made me laugh and books that made me feel I could be anything I wanted to be." So when she decided to write about kids in the crowded city, she wanted to make the book funny. Right away the idea of a duck in an elevator popped into her head. "Yeah, I thought, that would be pretty funny!" Mrs. Berends has written other children's stories and also a book for adults, *Whole Child, Whole Parent*. She lives with her husband and two sons in Hastings-on-Hudson, New York.

About the Illustrator

DIANE WORFOLK ALLISON studied art and literature at Macalester College and later became a Montessori teacher. She lives in Brookline, Massachusetts, with her husband and two children. Besides illustrating children's books, she teaches art to elementary school children as part of the Massachusetts artist-in-residence program.

Do you like books about animals?
You may also want to read

Absolutely Lucy
By Ilene Cooper

Bobby's mother smiled. "Now it's time for your special present," she said.

His father said, "Close your eyes."

Bobby was glad to close his eyes. It would be easier to look surprised when he opened them.

"Okay, Bobby," his father called, "you can look!"

Bobby opened his eyes. He didn't have to pretend to be surprised. Or happy. In his father's arms was a puppy. The cutest, squirmiest little dog Bobby had ever seen.